Frederick McSnoogle and the
Monster Named Dread

Frederick McSnoogle and the Monster Named Dread

Annette Proctor

RESOURCE *Publications* · Eugene, Oregon

FREDERICK MCSNOOGLE AND THE MONSTER NAMED DREAD

Resource Publications
An Imprint of Wipf and Stock Publishers
199 W. 8th Ave., Suite 3
Eugene, OR 97401

www.wipfandstock.com

PAPERBACK ISBN: 978-1-5326-7504-1
HARDCOVER ISBN: 978-1-5326-7505-8
EBOOK ISBN: 978-1-5326-7506-5

Manufactured in the U.S.A.

Prologue:

Most little children sincerely suspect
there are monsters around
      that only kids can detect.

Stories tell us monsters are fun and happy,
have colorful fur
      and act kind of sappy.

But children like Frederick, they know for sure
some monsters aren't funny
      wearing bright colored fur.

Frederick's monster wasn't playful or kind,
he lived in his pocket
      and played in his mind.

His monster was tricky, he could shrink very small;
or suddenly grow huge
      very scary and tall.

Dread was this monster's mean name,
and being mean
      was his very mean game.

*Psalm 27:1 The Lord is my light and my salvation;
whom shall I fear or dread? The Lord is the refuge and
stronghold of my life; of whom shall I be afraid?*

Frederick McSnoogle

"My hands are sweaty and so is my head,"
cried Frederick McSnoogle,
    just call him Fred.

"I'm worried and anxious, in an awful stew,
school starts tomorrow
    oh what will I do?"

"What if some kids call me mean names?
What if something breaks
    and I get the blame?"

"What if I'm not smart and can't learn to read?
What if my backpack doesn't have
    all that I need?"

"What if I forget what comes after five?
I'm a goner for sure,
    I'll never survive."

"What if I get lost on the way to the school?
Kids might point and laugh,
    I'd feel like a fool."

"Mom! I think I'm really too young:
you need me around,
        we can have lots of fun."

"The dog will be lonely and so will the cat,
they'll think that I'm dead.
        they won't know where I'm at."

"The weather is freezing, I'll catch a terrible cold;
then my stiff lifeless body
        is all that you'll hold."

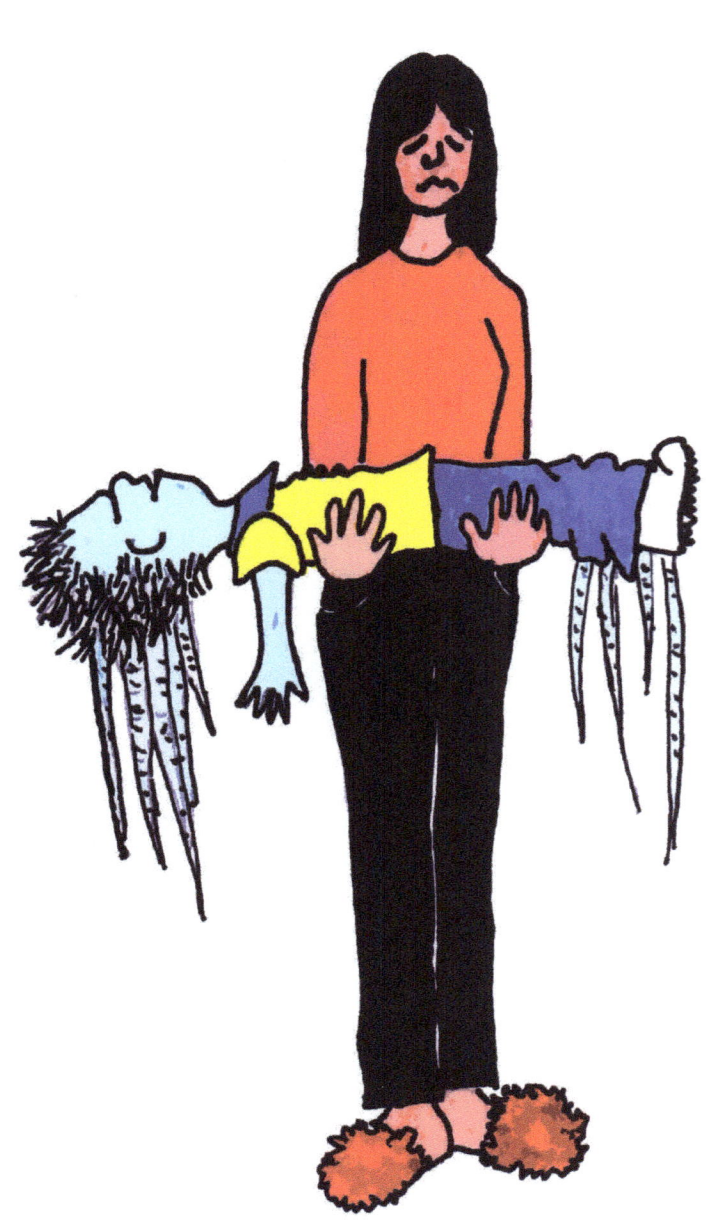

"I just remembered, school is not what I need.
Mom! You can teach me to count,
    you can teach me to read."

A monster in Fred's pocket started to grow large.
Fred didn't know it but
    the monster was in charge.

Yes little Frederick had exhausted his brain,
his thinking was fuzzy,
    his excuses were lame.

His mother took Frederick gently by his hand,
they walked through the door
     and climbed into their van.

Mom in her voice so gentle and kind,
said, "Let us just pray
     for peace in your mind."

Suddenly the monster began to think,
"Oh crum! Oh dear!
     I'm beginning to shrink."

"That prayer just ruined my game,
for being mean is my job
     and Dread is my name."

The school room was colorful and full of kids just Fred's size.
The teacher was smiling;
    what a pleasant surprise.

Then the monster started to shrink very fast.
A prayer had ruined him,
    his game couldn't last.

Frederick came home and burst through the door,
"Mom! I met some kids,
    Claude, Butch and Eleanore."

"We played lots of games and I counted to TEN!
Mom, please don't stop me,
    can I PLEASE go again?"

Psalm 56: 11 In God I have put my trust; I will not be afraid.

Tests

Frederick ran home, he ran all the way.
There was something important,
     that he wanted to say.

"Mom!" he hollered, "something terrible at school,
I just heard the news
     from two guys that are cool."

Frederick was breathing hard, he needed a rest,
"Mom!" he choked "Mom!
     We're going to have TESTS!"

Frederick collapsed and he fell to the floor;
pounding his fists,
     "I CAN'T TAKE IT ANYMORE!"

Listen carefully, you might even hear
a voice from his pocket
     starting to cheer.

Frederick stood up to pace around the room.
His face was pale and
        had an expression of gloom.

Muttering to himself, "I may not survive,
don't they know
        I'm only just five?"

The monster by now was flying around the room,
tossing worries like confetti
        as up and down he zoomed.

Mother's answer was soft but her voice sounded firm,
"Frederick dear, calm down,
        remember what you've learned.

You're upset, your thinking is blurry,
in God's own book
        He tells us not to worry."

The clouds of confetti all fell to the floor;
the pocket monster cried,
    "This isn't fun anymore."

Frederick began to get some control about then,
he remained very quiet
    and practiced counting to ten.

A thought suddenly bubbled up in Fred's young mind,
"What IS a test?
    I don't even know," he whined.

Psalm 94: 19 In the multitude of my anxious thoughts
within me, Your comforts cheer and delight my soul.

P. E.

"Now children," the teacher said out of the blue,
"Now children, today we're
    doing something new."

Frederick immediately began to frown,
that word "new" scared him,
    and made his heart pound.

Something in his pocket started to move and to wiggle,
something in his pocket
    began to smile and to giggle.

The monster's old game had started again,
that kind of nastiness
    you wouldn't do to a friend.

What ifs began to stir in Fred's little mind.
A new list of worries
    of a different kind.

Muttering to himself with his voice quite low,
those fears of the unknown
    began to grow.

"What if I can't do this thing, this thing that is new?
What if it's confusing
    and I don't have a clue?"

"What if I'm embarrassed? My face will turn red,
I want to go home,
    and be in my bed."

I'll go under the covers and curl up in a ball.
No one will notice,
they won't miss me at all.

The teacher's mouth opened, she continued to speak,
Frederick tried to act brave
but his knees felt so weak.

"Today dear children, we're going to the gym.
You're going to have P. E.,
with Mr. Muscleytrim."

"P. E.! Oh no!" Frederick groaned and then sighed,
"I hate not knowing
what I haven't even tried."

The monster called Dread grew large having a wonderful time,
he especially enjoyed it when
Frederick would whine.

But his joy lasted just a short time,
for it was his turn,
    the monster's turn to whine.

"Oh no!" cried the monster, "this isn't cool,
Fred's remembered a verse,
    he learned in Sunday School."

In a straight line and down the school hall
the children walked,
    the short and the tall.

The class marched through a big metal door.
The room was quite large
    with a shiny wood floor.

Frederick's knees felt stronger as he entered the gym.
There were balls and hoops,
    there was Mr. Muscleytrim.

Kids were running and jumping, kids were playing a game.
Kids were calling to him,
    they were calling his name.

The monster named Dread cried out loud moans.
He twisted and turned
    and groaned low groans.

Not only that, that wasn't all,
that monster had shrunk,
    he'd shrunk very small.

A ball flew toward Frederick that he reached up and caught.
I think I can do this
    little Fred thought.

Psalm 119: 105 Your word is a lamp to my feet and a light to my path.

The Bus

"Now is the time," Frederick's mother had said,
"Now is the time," as Frederick
    climbed into his bed.

"To go on the bus that will take you to school.
Riding the bus will be fun.
    Riding the bus will be cool."

Riding the bus isn't cool thought little Fred.
Riding the bus is scary
    and it's just what I 'Dread'.

McSnoogle was startled by the visions in his head.
His eyes were wide open
    as he laid in his bed.

What was mom thinking, was she out of her mind?
I'm not ready for this,
    what excuse can I find?

Frederick was worried and didn't even know
that old monster Dread
          had begun to grow.

The what ifs had arrived, that poor little kid,
it had started again
          as it usually did.

What if there's no place for me to sit?
I don't like this bus idea,
          I don't like it one little bit.

What if the big kids on the bus are tough?
Doesn't mom know
          I have worries enough?

What if there's no one for me to sit by?
My chin might shake,
    I might even cry.

What if I miss the bus when it's time to go home?
I'd be stuck at school
    all by myself all alone!

What if I forget to get off at my stop?
Will they know what to do?
    Would they go get a cop?

The monster by this time had filled the room;
happy with himself
    at Frederick's dark gloom

Things seemed very dark that particular night;
then through the window
    came the moon's shimmering light.

The moonlight seemed to clear Fred's head.
"I KNOW what to do,"
    as he sat up in his bed.

Frederick McSnoogle then knelt by his bed,
and a short little prayer
      that five year old said.

That made the old monster just quiver and moan.
He shrunk a little smaller
      and groaned a low groan.

A miracle happened in the light of the moon.
A miracle that Frederick
      wouldn't forget very soon.

That pocket monster shriveled and shrank so fast,
he'd NEVER shrunk
      that fast in the past.

He'd shrunk so little, he'd shrunk so small,
there was hardly anything left,
      hardly anything at all.

*Psalm 116: 1, 2 I love the Lord because He has heard my
voice and supplications, because He has inclined His ear
to me, therefore will I call upon Him as long as I live.*

Epilogue:

Frederick grew up,
    he grew up very tall.
He still had some worries,
    some big and some small.

But that old monster of his,
    mostly left him alone.
Frederick knew what to do,
    and the monster found a new home.

I John 4: 16, 18 God is love . . . perfect love drives out fear.